GERALDINE McCAUGHREAN

Father and Son

ILLUSTRATED BY

FABIAN NEGRIN

h
Hodder
Children's
Books

A division of Hachette Children's Books

AFTER THE STAR HAD SET, after the angels had roosted, after the shepherds had hurried back to their sheep, there was one person still awake in the dark stable.

Father and Son

For the angelic host of FCB - G.M.

Father and Son

by Geraldine McCaughrean and Fabian Negrin

First published in hardback in 2006
This paperback edition first published in 2007
by Hodder Children's Books

Text copyright © Geraldine McCaughrean 2006
Illustrations copyright © Fabian Negrin 2006

Hodder Children's Books
338 Euston Road, London NW1 3BH

Hodder Children's Books Australia
Level 17/207 Kent Street
Sydney, NSW 2000

A catalogue record of this book is available from the British Library.

ISBN: 978 0 340 88209 2

Printed in China

Hodder Children's Books is a division of Hachette Children's Books.
An Hachette Livre UK Company.

Joseph sat watching the baby asleep
in a manger of straw.

"Mine, but not mine," he whispered.
"How am I supposed to stand in for
your real Father? How is a simple
man like me to bring up the Son
of God?

Not a good start. I could not even
find him a proper place to be born,
a proper bed to sleep in – He who
has cradled us all in his hands since
the Start of Time.

What lullabies should I sing to someone who taught the angels to dance and peppered the sky with songbirds?

How can I teach him his words and letters: he who strung the alphabet together, he who whispered dreams into a million, million ears, in a thousand different languages.

The very thought of it leaves me speechless.

How can I teach him the Scriptures?
It will be like reading him a book he
wrote himself!

What stories can I tell him? He wrote
the whole history of the world.

What jokes? He knows them all.

Didn't he invent the hilarious
hippopotamus and make the rivers
gurgle with laughter?

Didn't he form the first face, wink
and make it smile?

Someone tell me: how do I protect
a child whose arm brandished the
first bolt of lightning, who lobbed
the first thunderclap, who wears
sunlight for armour, and a helmet
of stars?

And yet... and yet... somehow my
heart quakes for you, child, small
as you are.

How shall I teach you Right and Wrong, when it was YOU who drew up the rules, YOU who parted Good from Bad?

How?

When I get angry and lose my temper, who will be to blame? Always me, I suppose.

How do I feed and clothe someone
who seeded the oceans with fish
and hung up fruit in the trees,
who shod the camels and crowned
the deer?

It's bread and fishes from now on,
son, and clothes no better than mine.

What games shall we play, boy, you and I? I mean, how can you rough-and-tumble with someone who pinned the ocean in place with a single, tack-headed moon?

And how shall I ever astound you,
child, as my father did me.
You are the one who fitted the
chicken into the egg and the oak
tree into an acorn!

How can I put a roof over your head,
knowing it was you who glass-roofed
the world and thatched the sky with
clouds, and stitched the snow with
threads of melting silver?

I am a carpenter, child. By rights,
you should learn my trade.
But how can I teach you to plane
a door knowing it was you who
planed the plains, who carved
the valleys and hewed the hills,
the wind in your one hand and
rain in the other?

How?

What presents can I offer you who
has already given me everything?
  This wife.
  This night.
  This happiness.
  This son.

What shall I pass down to you,
little one, apart from a world of
Love? Not as much as the colour
of my eyes. Not even my name.

  And yet... I've been thinking, child...

My hands
are strong,
God knows.
And everyone
needs an
extra pair
of hands
from time
to time.

So that's
what I'll give
you, son.
That's what
I'll be —
God willing.
A helping
hand."

So, long after the star had set,
after the angels had roosted,
after the shepherds had hurried
back to their sheep, there was
one person still awake in the dark
stable, watching over a sleeping
child...

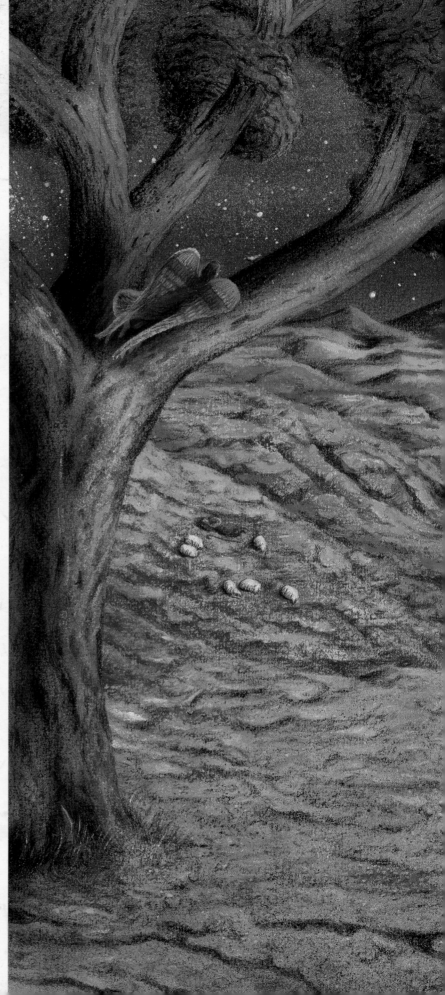

...while his God watched over him.